The ADVENTURES of CHARLIE

The Mummy

OR
ANOTHER GREAT USE FOR TOILET PAPER

Evans

First published in the UK in 2010 by
Evans Brothers Limited
2A Portman Mansions
Chiltern Street
London
W1U 6NR

First published in the USA in 2009 by
Marshall Cavendish Corporation,
Tarrytown, NY
Text and Illustration copyright © 2009 by Steve Shreve

British Library Cataloguing in Publication Data
Shreve, Steve.
        The mummy, or, Another great use for toilet paper.
        (The adventures of Charlie)
        1. Charlie (Fictitious character: Shreve) Juvenile fiction.
        2. Mummies--Juvenile fiction.
        3. Adventure stories.
        4. Children's stories.
        I. Title II. Series III. Another great use for toilet paper
        813.6-dc22

ISBN-13: 9780237542856

Printed in China

VISIT OUR WEBSITE
Evans
www.evansbooks.co.uk

The ADVENTURES of CHARLIE

The Mummy

OR
ANOTHER GREAT USE FOR TOILET PAPER

by

Steve Shreve

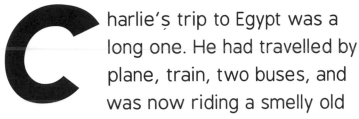

Charlie's trip to Egypt was a long one. He had travelled by plane, train, two buses, and was now riding a smelly old camel with bad breath into the desert. He couldn't wait to help his Uncle Howard, an archaeologist, excavate a mummy for the local museum back home.

When Charlie finally arrived, he hopped off the camel. "Hi, Uncle Howard."

"Charlie!" his uncle called out. "I hope you're ready to get to work!"

"Work?" Charlie asked.

"Work," answered Uncle Howard.

Uncle Howard wasted no time in loading
Charlie up with a big rucksack full of
heavy excavation gear — shovels, a
pickaxe, a crowbar, rope, and a roll of
toilet paper, because you never know
when a roll of toilet paper might come
in handy.

Soon, Charlie found himself trudging
off into the hot desert in search of an
ancient pyramid.

After many hours of walking, they came
to a stop.

"Here we are!" bellowed Uncle Howard.

"This is it?" Charlie asked. "It's not very big."

"Don't let looks deceive you," replied
his uncle.

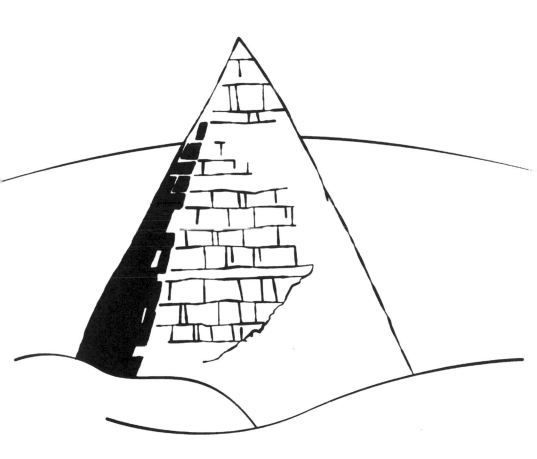

Charlie helped his uncle pry open the stone door with the crowbar, and they stepped into the darkness.

Uncle Howard turned on a torch and led them down a flight of stairs. He swung the light around the basement room until it settled on a sarcophagus in the corner. Uncle Howard lifted the heavy lid and moved it to the side.

"Eureka! We have discovered the long-lost tomb of King Butthankhamen," Uncle Howard announced. "Better known to the world as King Butt!"

"He looks like a King Butt," Charlie agreed. "Hey – what's that pinned to his chest?"

"I say! It looks like some sort of note," said Uncle Howard.

Uncle Howard unpinned the note and explained that it was written in ancient hieroglyphics. He began to decipher the message.

"Beware!" he read. "Whoever disturbs this tomb will invoke the wrath of King Butthankhamen and be cursed to – "

Uncle Howard stopped.

"Cursed?" Charlie shouted. "Cursed to what?"

"I can't tell," his uncle replied. "There's some sort of large, brown stain covering the rest."

"Yuck," said Charlie. "It's not his brains, is it? I heard they used to pull a mummy's brains out through his nose when they were mummifying him."

"Don't be silly," Uncle Howard said. "His brains are in that jar over there. It's probably just his spleen or something."

"Oh," said Charlie. "That's not so bad, I guess."

Suddenly, the door at the top of the stairs closed with a great **CRASH!**

"Oh, bother," said Uncle Howard. "I do believe we're trapped."

"It's the curse!" said Charlie.

"Nonsense," said Uncle Howard. "There's no such thing as a – "

Uncle Howard was cut off by a scraping sound behind them. Together, they *slooowly* turned around.

"Crikey!" exclaimed Uncle Howard.
"It's the mummy!"

King Butt staggered forward.

"Run, Charlie!" Uncle Howard cried.

Charlie ran, but with the exit sealed,
there was no hope of escape.

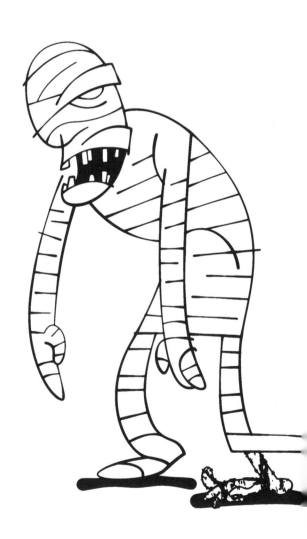

If I can't get out, Charlie thought, *I'll have to stop that mummy.*

Charlie ran up behind King Butt, grabbed a loose bandage, and tied it to a large piece of fallen stone.

But Charlie hadn't counted on the mummy's strength.

The large rock didn't even slow King Butt down. He just kept moving towards Uncle Howard as his bandages began to unravel.

Then, Charlie got an even better idea.

"Hey!" Charlie yelled. "Your shoelace is untied!"

King Butt looked down.

Charlie and his uncle Howard sprinted down the tunnel – further into the pyramid.

They ran through a maze of corridors
and stopped to rest around a bend.

"I don't hear anything," Charlie noted.
"Maybe he left."

They carefully peeked around
the corner.

The mummy was still far away, but he
was slowly moving towards them.

"Wow," said Charlie. "I thought he'd
be faster."

"He is four thousand years old, you
know," replied Uncle Howard. "But . . .
he'll catch up eventually."

"So what do we do now?" asked Charlie.

Uncle Howard looked around. "Quick –
into this little room," he ordered.

They went into a room off the corridor
and quietly pulled the door closed
behind them.

"It sure is dark in here," Charlie observed.

Uncle Howard lit a match. "Not to worry you," he said, "but we're not alone in this room."

Charlie looked around. "Aaah!" he shouted. **"Snakes!"**

They started back towards the door, but it was too late – they heard a noise outside.

"Now what?" asked Charlie. "King Butt has caught up with us!"

"Oh, I wouldn't worry too much about him," said Uncle Howard. "The snakes will probably finish us off long before he gets in."

Fortunately, most of the snakes weren't poisonous. Keeping the snakes from crawling into their socks was the worst Charlie and his Uncle Howard had to deal with.

After a while, they even stopped worrying about King Butt. The mummy was so busy pushing on the door to get in that he never thought to try pulling it.

Charlie and his uncle had one new problem, though – after all of that running, they were starting to feel a little hungry.

"You know," said Charlie, "maybe we could solve our hunger problem *and* keep those pesky snakes out of our socks."

"What do you mean?" asked Uncle Howard.

"Let's build a fire and cook 'em!"

"Great idea, Charlie, my boy," said Uncle Howard. He pulled a box of matches out of his shirt pocket.

It wasn't too long before they were enjoying a nice, hot snake dinner.

"Not too bad, once you get used to the taste," said Uncle Howard.

"And the chewiness," added Charlie.

After a few more snakes, Charlie and his Uncle Howard were starting to feel at home. But just as they got comfortable, they heard King Butt *pulling* the door open.

"Uh-oh," said Charlie.

King Butt entered the small room. He was almost completely unravelled now and didn't look too happy about it.

"This is it," said Uncle Howard. "I'm afraid it's the curse for us."

"Oh, well. We were almost out of snakes anyway," said Charlie.

Step by plodding step, the mummy
drew closer.

Charlie could barely watch as King Butt
approached him. Then the mummy reached
out, grabbed his underpants,
and YANKED!

"Aaaah!" Charlie yelled. "Wedgie!"

Uncle Howard was no luckier. "My
underpants!" he bellowed.

The curse now fulfilled, King Butt just stood there.

"What do we do now?" said Charlie.

"I don't know," replied his uncle. "The museum will never stand for an unravelled mummy."

"Yeah," agreed Charlie. "He looks like a shrivelled sausage."

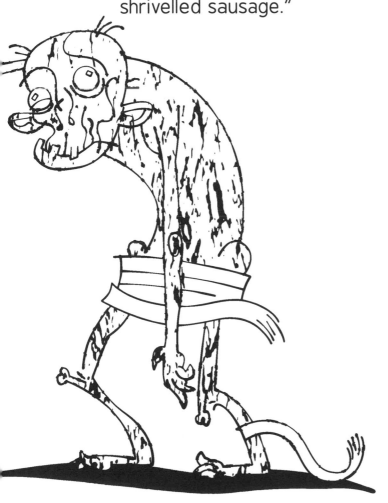

Charlie and Uncle Howard tried their best to rewrap King Butthankhamen, but it was no use — his bandages were completely ruined.

"We'll have to bring him like this," said Uncle Howard with a sigh.

"Wait a minute," Charlie said, "didn't we pack a roll of toilet paper before we left?"

Uncle Howard considered this for a moment. "It's worth a try, I suppose."

Charlie and his uncle quickly wrapped King Butt in toilet paper and bundled him off to the airport.

There wasn't much to do on the long flight, so Charlie tried to chat with King Butt. But unfortunately, mummies aren't really great conversationalists.

Finally, Charlie and his Uncle Howard arrived at the museum and dropped off King Butt.

The curator looked at the mummy strangely, but he didn't say anything.

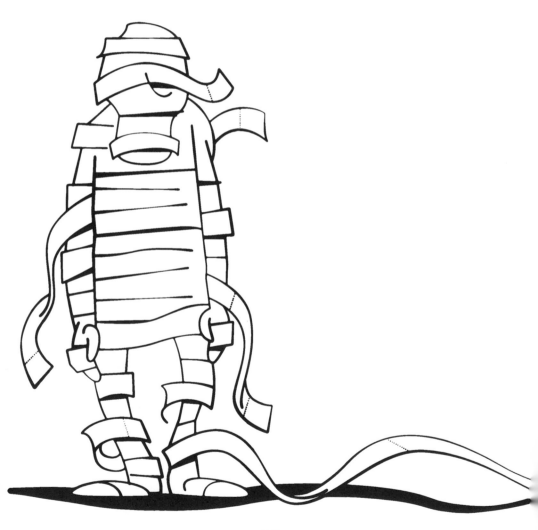

Charlie had just one more thing he had to do before going home.

He tore a long piece of toilet paper off King Butt and headed towards the toilet.